AMA:
BABiES

For Rupert
P. & E.R.

For Esther and Maxwell
D.S.

First published in 1990
Text copyright © Paul and Emma Rogers, 1990
Illustrations copyright © Dee Shulman, 1990

All rights reserved
Printed in England
for J.M. Dent & Sons Ltd
91 Clapham High Street
London SW4 7TA

British Library Cataloguing in Publication Data
Rogers, Paul *1950–*
    Amazing babies.
    I. Title   II. Rogers, Emma   III. Shulman, Dee
    823.914

ISBN 0–460–88030–6

AMAZING BABIES

Paul & Emma Rogers

ILLUSTRATED BY DEE SHULMAN

Dent Children's Books
London

Amazing

Some babies are greedy. Some are shy. Others are noisy or naughty or a little bit lively. You probably know babies like that. But just wait till you meet the babies in this book!

Take Billy Buzoni. Greedy isn't the word for it! Wherever, *when*ever he sees food, he simply gobbles it down. And Billy isn't the only amazing baby in town.

Just round the corner from Billy live the Springers. Some babies are bouncy. But when the Springers' baby arrived – little Pat – they could

Babies

see she wasn't just bouncy. She was a born acrobat!

And what about Mary MacNab! So contrary she *never* does *anything* she's told – and *always* does *every-thing* she's told not to.

Then up the road lives little De-lilah Pie. There's never been a baby who was so painfully shy – or so clever at hiding.

Nearby are the Hollers, with their baby, Rory. He could scream so loud that – Well, you'd better read the stories ...

Billy

the unbelievably greedy baby

Billy, the Unbelievably Greedy Baby

Right from the day he was born, Billy Buzoni ate enough food for twenty babies and more. He'd have potatoes, porridge, plums, bread, bananas, beans, soup, spaghetti and ice-cream – and that was only his breakfast.

Billy ate seven meals a day – and snacks in between. Everyone thought he was the greediest baby they'd ever met. Poor Mr and Mrs Buzoni didn't know what to do.

As soon as Billy learned to grab, they hardly dared take him out shopping.

Once Billy started to crawl, they had to put a padlock on the fridge ... And within a week of his learning to walk, they had to keep the food on the highest shelf in the larder ...

As for a visit to the fair, it was a nightmare for his parents ...

At the end of a meal, it was no good saying, "No more now." A few minutes later they'd find Billy munching a magazine or chewing up flowers outside.

One day Mr Buzoni came in from the garden and called to Mrs Buzoni:

"You know the rabbit's been getting thinner. Well, guess who's been enjoying its dinner."

In the end, they were so worried they took Billy along to the hospital. But while they were talking to the doctor, he got into the hospital kitchens. Lots of the patients went hungry that day . . .

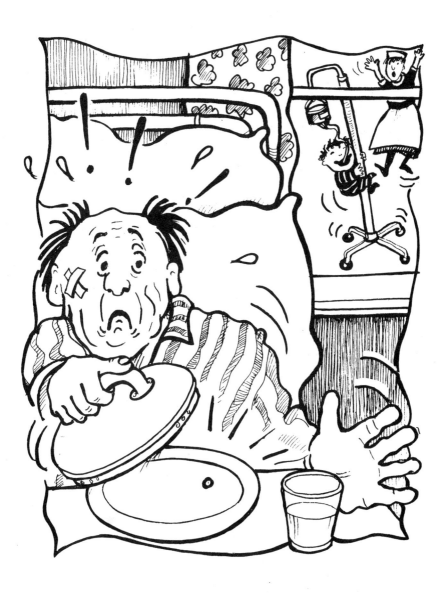

Billy Buzoni was eating his family out of house and home. Mrs Buzoni stared at the empty larder. There was only one lettuce leaf left on the shelf. They were down to their last stick of spaghetti. They had only a few pennies left to spend. What *were* they going to do?

Then, on the way to the supermarket, they saw a notice:

PANCAKE EATING COMPETITION
THE OLD TOWN HALL, NEW ROAD
FIRST PRIZE £1,000!!

For a moment, both the Buzonis thought, "How very silly!" Then their eyes met and in one breath they cried, "We'll enter Billy!"
The very next day they started Billy's training. It was hard work for his mum and dad, but life for Billy was wonderful – just one meal after another!

In between, they took him for long walks to build up his appetite. And after each meal, when Billy appeared to have finished, instead of saying,

"Quick! Let's hide what's left from his sight!" they begged:

"You can do it, Billy, just one more bite!"

"Funny," Billy thought,

"I wonder why it's pancakes again tonight?"

The day of the competition came. A huge crowd had gathered. Poor Billy hadn't eaten all day. Mr and Mrs Buzoni sat him at a table. At last they heard the umpire say:

"All right. No resting. No one must cheat. You must keep going. Ready … Steady … Eat! …"

Cynthia Stodge got off to a good start, stuffing them in four at a time ... And Big Bob was washing them down with mouthfuls of beer ... The crowd cheered. The cooks kept the pancakes coming ...

But what's this? Big Bob was slowing down! And Cynthia was falling asleep!

"Come on!" the crowd shouted.

"You mustn't stop yet!

You've got to win. We've all made a bet!"

But Big Bob wasn't looking too good.

"Oh, my tummy," he groaned. "I feel so ill.

I can't eat any more – but that baby will!"

Mr Buzoni just smiled to his wife and whispered, "Keep munching, Bill."

The crowd kept count as the pancakes disappeared.

"A hundred and two? It can't be true!
Two hundred and four!
He's asking for more!"
The umpire stood up.
"He's only a baby," he said. "Just a beginner.
But I declare Billy Buzoni THE WINNER!"

Mr and Mrs Buzoni gave Billy a big hug — very carefully. The umpire presented them with a cheque for a thousand pounds. He asked the Buzonis what they'd do with the money. Take a holiday? Buy a car?

Mr Buzoni replied:

"We might have a treat or two, maybe,
But most of the prize will buy food for the baby!"

That night the Buzonis went to the best restaurant in town to celebrate. They ordered the grandest meal on the menu — fresh lobster, roast beef, raspberry sorbet, trifle and cheese.

And Billy — couldn't eat a thing.

Pat

the incredibly acrobatic baby

Pat, the Incredibly Acrobatic Baby

Look, the moon has a smile on its face. But do you know why?

It all began when Mr and Mrs Springer's little girl was born.

"Aahh!" said the nurse. "What strong legs and feet!

A real bouncing baby, isn't she sweet!"

And it was true. Pat bounced everywhere. She bounced on her mother and father's lap. She bounced in her cot as if it were a trampoline. Mr and Mrs Springer laughed and clapped. And the more they clapped the more Pat bounced.

It wasn't long before the baby learned to swing. She swung from the towel rail. She swung from the bannisters. She swung like a monkey from the handle of her pram. Wherever she went, people stopped and stared. At the supermarket they gaped as Pat practised walking on her hands, picking her way between packets and tins on the moving belt at the checkout.

"Fancy allowing the child to do that!

Letting her act like an acrobat!"

But her mother just smiled and said,

"Clever girl, Pat!"

24

In the evening, Mr and Mrs Springer would tell each other proudly what Pat had done that day.

Her father would say:

"Her favourite thing in the park is the trees.

She thinks every branch is a flying trapeze!"

Her mother would say:

"She loves that big crane in the middle of town.

It took five workmen to get her down."

Occasionally, Pat got into a little trouble. One day when her granny had been looking after her, Mrs Springer found her covered in soot from head to foot.

"What's she been up to, to get so black?" asked Mrs Springer.

"Up to the chimney-pots and back!" said Pat's granny.

Not long after, the next-door neighbour came round to complain, carrying a broken washing-line. She told Mrs Springer that Pat had used it for a tight-rope.

"She was half-way across when the line went snap!"

"How clever! I hope you remembered to clap!" said Pat's mother.

Mr and Mrs Springer were never very cross. They thought themselves lucky to have such an acrobatic baby. Until, that is, they took Pat to see a gymnastics display.

At first she sat wide-eyed on her mother's lap. Then she began to bounce and shriek and clap her hands. Suddenly she was away! Before the performers knew it, Pat was in there amongst them, swinging and leaping from bar to bar.

Soon everyone stood open-mouthed in amazement: the baby was a natural gymnast! When at last Pat landed on the crash mat amidst a storm of applause, the trainer rushed up to Mr and Mrs Springer, and said:

"The child's a sensation! The star of the show! She'd win the Olympics! You *must* let her go!"

But Mr and Mrs Springer said:

"No."

Pat was very sad. Her mother and father tried to explain.

"You're much too young for a life like that." said Mrs Springer.

"Gymnastics is far too dangerous, Pat," Mr Springer added.

So life in the Springer's house returned to normal – for a while. Then one day Pat went missing. One minute she was riding the dog around the garden, the next she was gone. Mrs Springer looked in all the usual places, along the garden fence, on the garage roof, but there was no sign of her. Then the girl next door owned up.

"Pat had this lolly. She gave me a lick,
In return for a go on my pogo stick."

The Springers didn't know what to do. They were at their wits' end. Mr Springer was about to call the police when the phone rang. It was someone from the Space Station.

"Your baby's with us. Please come here fast.

We've just got her down from the radio mast!"

Yes, Pat had bounced all the way there – boing! boing! – on the pogo stick!

When the Springers arrived, the Commander-in-Chief was waiting for them at the gates.

"Good evening," he said. "Have you ever thought
Of making your daughter an astronaut?"
The Springers shook their heads.

"We know our Pat is ever so frisky,
But wouldn't that be just a teeny bit risky?"
"Heck no!" said the Commander-in-Chief.
"She'll float like a bubble. There's nowhere to fall.
You've nothing to worry about at all."
Pat looked at her parents. Her eyes said "Please!"
The Commander-in-Chief said:
"The baby's a marvel! She's just what we need.
With her, our space mission is sure to succeed!"
So Mr and Mrs Springer had to agree.

A few weeks later they went to
watch the launch. A crowd
of thousands had gathered
at the space station.
  "Five ... four ... three ...
two ... one ... zero ...
BLAST OFF!"

That evening, millions of people all over the world stared at their televisions in amazement at the sight of little Pat in her tiny space suit up among the stars, doing swoops and triple turns, spirals and loop-the-loops. Her mother and father clapped and cheered:

"She's famous! The very first baby in space!"

So that's why the moon has a smile on its face!

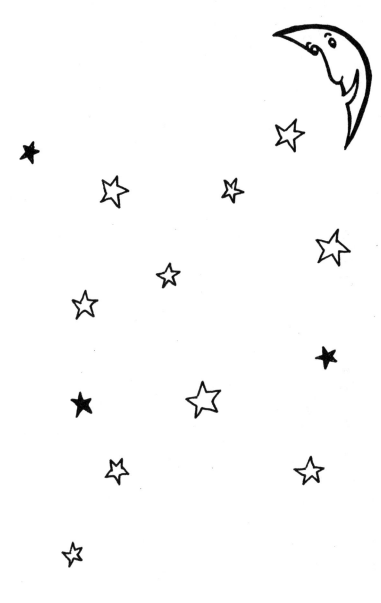

Mary, *the terribly contrary baby*

Mr and Mrs MacNab owned the corner Post Office. When baby Mary was born, they kept her in her pram behind the counter so all the customers could see her.

"Two first-class stamps and a stick of glue.
And hello Mary! Peek-a-boo!"
they'd say, peering over at her.

Sometimes her mum and dad took her out of the pram and carried her round. Sometimes they sat her on their lap while they served the customers. But as she grew bigger, she *would* grab things – especially things she wasn't meant to.

Mr MacNab got rather cross. His wife said:
"She's only little. She's not very old.
Babies never do what they're told."

But as Mary grew older, it wasn't just that she didn't do what she was told. She actually did the *opposite* ... like licking whole sheets of stamps ... and swapping the price tags on things in the window ... and scribbling 'M' for Mary on all the birthday cards in the rack! Mr and Mrs MacNab seemed to spend all day saying:

"Stop it! Don't *do* that! Please Mary, NO!"
but it didn't make any difference and at last they decided,

"It's no use! It's hopeless! She'll just have to go!"

Next day, Mrs MacNab and Mary went... to Playgroup. By lunchtime, Mr MacNab thought he'd had a busy morning serving customers. But that was nothing compared with what poor Mrs MacNab had been doing. She staggered in exhausted.

"Mary was dreadful! Whatever I said,
She just did the opposite instead!"

That night, the MacNabs lay awake, trying to think what they could do. Suddenly, Mrs Mac-Nab had an idea.

"We know we can't force her, she'd just make a scene.
So let's tell her to *do* what we really *don't* mean!"

Next day, Mrs MacNab and Mary went to Play-group again. As soon as Mary began to be naughty in the Wendy House, Mrs MacNab called to her:

"Is that Sally's dolly? Well don't give it back! Look – Harry's not crying. He needs a good smack!"

When they brought out the climbing frame and slide, Mrs MacNab smiled at Mary and said:

"It's no fun taking turns. Give Sharon a shove. Then you can slide by yourself, Mary love!"

At breaktime, Mrs MacNab sat beside Mary at a little table. They'd been making pretend cakes.

"I'd eat all that Play-doh if I were you," said her mother. And when they came round with the real mid-morning snack, she added,

"Only one biscuit? You could grab two!"

Afterwards they went over to the art corner.

"Why bother with paper," said Mrs MacNab.
"Just paint on the floor!
And snap all the crayons – what else are they
for?"

Mary finished her picture. It was time to go
home. All the children were helping to tidy up.
Mrs MacNab said to Mary:

"That's right! Leave the Lego all over the
place.
Now don't say goodbye – just pull a rude
face!"

The other mothers looked appalled. But it had
worked! Mary had done exactly the opposite
to what her mother had asked her. She'd taken
turns on the slide, shared the toys, been ever
so helpful – and nice to everyone!

Soon Mary's parents had got the hang of how to handle their contrary baby. From time to time, they reminded each other:

"Remember to think what you're trying to say.

And keep all important things out of her way!" Like the key to the safe, which hung on a little hook high up behind the counter.

One particularly busy morning, before setting off for Playgroup, Mrs MacNab was helping Mr MacNab in the Post Office. While no one was looking, Mary climbed onto her dad's stool and grabbed the key from its hook. It slipped from her hand and landed among a pile of papers. Down on her knees, Mary began searching furiously.

Just then, the Post Office door flew open! A strange looking man with a hanky tied round his face burst in. He carried a big plastic sack – and a gun!

"Hands up! Don't move! You won't get far!" he shouted.

"This is a hold-up! Stay where you are!"

Everyone froze, terrified. Everyone, that is, except Mary. Had she been told to do something?

"Stay where you are, did someone say?" thought Mary.

"Not likely! I'm going to Playgroup today!" And clutching the key, she crept along on her hands and knees to peep around the counter.

Mr and Mrs MacNab were forced to help the robber fill his sack. He was yelling at them:

"Quick as you can! All the parcels as well! And don't anyone touch that police alarm bell!"

Mary stood up. The robber still hadn't seen her.

"What mustn't I touch?" she thought. "This red button, you mean?

The last time I did that, it made Mummy scream!"

And giggling quietly, she reached up now and pressed the button.

Split seconds later, the whole place was vibrating with a wail like a giant-sized tomcat having his tail pulled. The robber panicked. He waved his arms wildly and shouted at the MacNabs:

"Right: All your money! Give it to me!"

But when Mr MacNab went to open the safe, he gasped to the robber:

"I don't know what's happened, I can't find the key!"

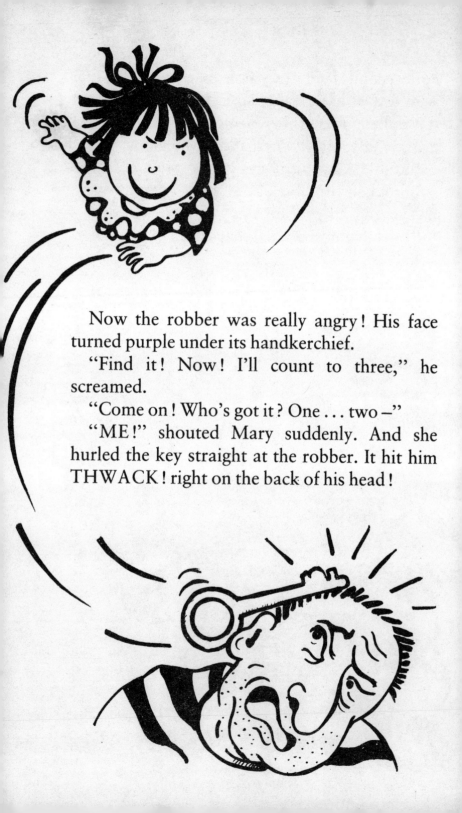

Now the robber was really angry! His face turned purple under its handkerchief.

"Find it! Now! I'll count to three," he screamed.

"Come on! Who's got it? One ... two –"

"ME!" shouted Mary suddenly. And she hurled the key straight at the robber. It hit him THWACK! right on the back of his head!

When the Police arrived, they found Mr and Mrs MacNab hugging their brave baby and grinning all over their faces.

"Magnificent Mary!" said the policeman, "You knocked him right out!"

"Oh, that isn't what we're so happy about," explained Mr and Mrs MacNab.

"No, something has happened that's totally new.

She's *done* something somebody *told* her to do!"

Delilah

the frightfully shy baby

Delilah, the Frightfully Shy Baby

Here are some photos of little Delilah Pie ...

There isn't much of her to be seen. Do you know why? Because Delilah's so terribly, terribly shy.

There are lots of pictures like these in the Pies' photograph album – of Delilah hiding behind trees or pulling a hat down over her eyes. She wouldn't play with other babies. She wouldn't even wave to them.

"Here's a nice little friend, say hello to Sam," said her mother.

"You're worse than a tortoise inside that pram!"

It was no better once Delilah learned to crawl. Whenever anyone came to see Mr or Mrs Pie, Delilah would hide behind the sofa or climb into one of the kitchen cupboards and close the door.

The Pies tried everything they could think of.

They took her for a picnic in the park – but she hid in a flowerbed. Mrs Pie tried to coax her out.

"A sandwich with soil in it's not nice to eat.
Come out and we'll have an ice-cream for a
treat!"

Delilah wouldn't budge. Mr Pie had a try. He
pointed at the sandpit.

"Look at the castles those children have made!
Wouldn't *you* like your own bucket and
spade?"

"It's worked!" they whispered.

Delilah came out from under the rose bushes
where some children had gathered to stare at
her. She crawled over to the sandpit with her
spade, dug a hole with it, then sat in the hole
with her bucket over her head.

One day, when Delilah was nearly two, Mr Pie was wondering what could be done.

"Perhaps what she needs is some sort of pet," he said.

"It might be worth trying, But what could we get?"
Mrs Pie was doubtful.

"We couldn't keep anything big in this flat.
Besides, she'd be scared of a dog or a cat."

The very next afternoon, on his way home from work, Mr Pie stopped at a pet shop. He arrived home with a big grin on his face. From behind his back he brought out a shoe-box with little holes in the lid.

"Don't be shy!" he said. "It's yours to keep.
Open the lid and have a peep."
Shelley was the perfect pet for Delilah. He was as shy as *she* was ... She had to wait an hour that first evening before he would even put his head out.

Until then, Delilah had never spoken to anybody except her mother and father. But now, little by little, day by day, she began talking to her tortoise.

Mr and Mrs Pie heard her talking in her bedroom.

"Lettuce for Shelley. Ooh, can't you go fast!"

They smiled to each other.

"She *is* coming out of her shell at last!"

Poor Shelley nearly wore himself out chasing backwards and forwards across the carpet after each lettuce leaf. He learned to scramble up steps, to scuttle along shelves. Delilah spent all her time training him. Soon he was the cleverest tortoise in town. He'd do almost anything for Delilah – and Delilah would do almost anything for *him*.

Christmas came. Mr and Mrs Pie decided to take Delilah to see a pantomime.

"It's all right, Delilah, you don't have to hide. No one will see you. It's all dark inside."

Delilah crept in to the theatre – though she wouldn't take off her coat. But then, who do you think was in her pocket?

The pantomime was *Cinderella*. The first half was fun. Then at the interval when the lights came on, Delilah tried hiding under her seat. But it kept tipping up, so she did a trick she'd learned from Shelley – and down went her head inside the collar of her coat.

After the interval, Prince Charming asked for some children to go up on stage to play games. Mr Pie whispered to Delilah:

"Wouldn't you like to go up too?

You could take your Shelley along with you!" Delilah shook her head and stuffed her hand into her pocket. Then, suddenly, her eyes opened wide. She got to her feet and walked towards the steps that led to the stage. Mr and Mrs Pie stared in amazement!

"Goodness! She's going! What brought this on?

She's going! She's going!! She's already gone!!!"

Delilah climbed onto the stage. Prince Charming came forward with his microphone.

"Hello young lady! What's your name?
Have you come up to join our game?"

But Delilah, with her coat over her head and only the tiniest crack left open, kept going – right to the back of the stage. The audience laughed as she disappeared behind the scenery. Then one tree wobbled dangerously and Delilah's face peeped out from among the paper leaves!

Mr Pie shouted:

"Come down, Delilah, come down! You'll fall!

That's not what you're meant to be doing at all!"

But little Delilah only climbed higher.

Prince Charming himself tried to see what was happening.

"There's something up there she's trying to get.

It looks like a tortoise!"

"It's Shelley, I bet!" cried Mr Pie.

Shelley had spotted the pretend leaves on the scenery and, thinking they would make a tasty snack, had scrabbled his way up to them.

Mrs Pie said faintly:

"Do something! Quickly. Make her stop!

Those leaves are shaking right at the top!"

A spotlight flashed across the trees. The audience gasped as they saw Delilah reaching up to grasp something from the catwalk high above the stage.

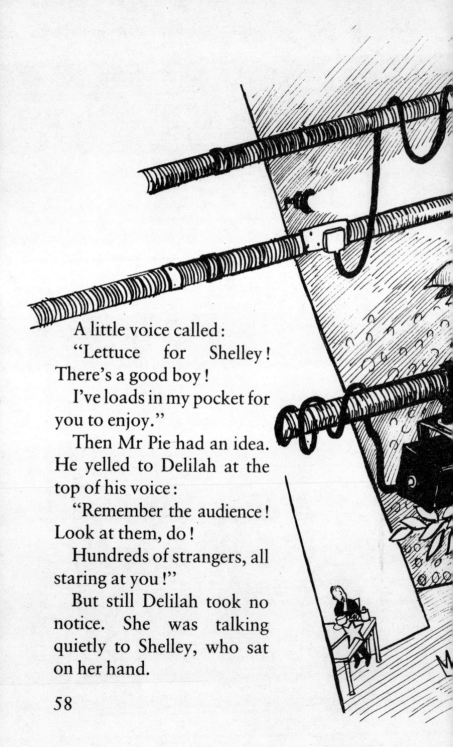

A little voice called:

"Lettuce for Shelley! There's a good boy!

I've loads in my pocket for you to enjoy."

Then Mr Pie had an idea. He yelled to Delilah at the top of his voice:

"Remember the audience! Look at them, do!

Hundreds of strangers, all staring at you!"

But still Delilah took no notice. She was talking quietly to Shelley, who sat on her hand.

"Silly old Shelley! These leaves aren't real!
It's time we went home for your evening
meal!"

Then a man with a ladder arrived, and Delilah
and Shelley were brought down safely. Mr Pie
turned to his wife.

"Ah well," he said, "She gave us a terrible
fright.

But she'll never be shy again after tonight!"

They were pleased when a photographer asked
for a picture of Delilah.

That week the photo he took appeared in the local paper. It showed Prince Charming and Cinderella presenting Delilah with three free tickets for the last performance of the pantomime. To this day, the Pies proudly keep a copy of it in their photograph album. Would you like to see it? Look!

Rory, the Deplorably Noisy Baby

Smash! Crash! What was that? It sounded like an elephant stampeding through a supermarket! But it wasn't.

Toot! Toot! Beep! Beep! What was that? It sounded like angry drivers in a traffic jam! But it wasn't.

Cling! Clang! Jangle! Bash! Twang! What was that? It sounded like a bandstand collapsing and all the musicians with all their instruments crashing through it! But it wasn't.

No, all that noise was made by just one baby!

Little Rory Holler had spent the morning playing in the kitchen . . .

in the garden . . .

and at the piano . . .

And all that noise was nothing compared to Rory's voice. For Rory had the loudest, shrillest, shriekiest voice ever.

His laugh rattled the plates on the dresser. His cry sent birds flying out of the trees. When Rory opened his mouth wide, the cat put its paws in its ears. When Rory screamed, even the dog couldn't hear itself howl.

Rory's mum and dad put up with his noisiness at home, but taking him out wasn't so easy. Mrs Holler never had to queue in the shops. As soon as Rory started to shout, everyone moved aside and said "After you." Poor Mrs Holler blushed as she whispered "Hush, Rory, do."

The summer approached and Rory was six months old. The Hollers decided they needed a holiday. Mrs Holler said:

"Let's fly to a sunny beach in Spain."

But Mr Holler said:

"What if he started to shout on the plane?"

They thought again.

After a while, Mr Holler said:

"Let's drive to that nice hotel we know."

But Mrs Holler shook her head.

"If Rory yelled, they'd ask us to go."

Surely there must be *something* they could do.

Yes! There was! They both
thought of it at once.

Five weeks later, the
Hollers poked cotton wool
in their ears and set off by
car for a lonely seaside cot-
tage. It was the perfect place
for Rory. He could bang and
bellow and shout, and no
one but his mum and dad
could hear him ...

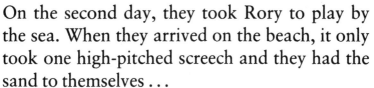

On the second day, they took Rory to play by
the sea. When they arrived on the beach, it only
took one high-pitched screech and they had the
sand to themselves ...

On the third day, they walked around the harbour. Rory roared with delight at the sight of the boats.

"I feel so embarrassed!" said Mrs Holler, as people stared. "There's nowhere to hide!"

Mr Holler whispered in Rory's ear:

"Be a good boy, and we'll go for a ride."

Rory grinned, silently. The Hollers hurried round to the sign at the quayside that said:

BOAT TRIPS daily

The boat rocked gently as Mrs Holler climbed aboard. Mr Holler passed her first Rory, then a bag full of things to help keep him quiet – buns, books, a dummy, a teddy bear, a strip of sticking plaster. Some were to eat and some were to play with, and some could be stuffed into – or over – Rory's mouth if he started screaming.

But, to his mum and dad's surprise, he didn't make a squeak. For a while he seemed quite entranced by the bobbing up and down of the boat and nearly nodded off to sleep. Then suddenly the engine started. Rory opened his mouth to yell, and at once it was filled with a large bun. By the time they were out of the harbour, they had already used all the buns and were trying to stop his screams with the dummy.

"I knew this would happen. We shouldn't have come!" said Mrs Holler.

"Rory will spoil it for everyone."

But then, as the boat chugged out to sea, Rory's eyes began to close.

"What a relief! He's having a nap.

If only he'd stay there, asleep on your lap," sighed Mr Holler.

The boat gently rocked. The baby slept. Then suddenly, the engine stopped. The skipper fumbled with rags and spanners but couldn't get it started. Everyone went quiet. All you could hear was the water slapping against the side of the boat and Rory snoring. As the wind blew them further and further out to sea, people were getting worried.

"We can't just sit here!"

"What can we do?"

"If someone could see us ..."

"Yes but *who*?"

There were no other boats in sight. The harbour was only a speck on the horizon.

At last a ship appeared in the distance. People waved coats and hankies, and the skipper waved a flag.

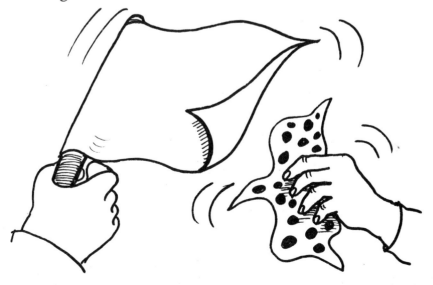

"AHOY!" one of them shouted. Two or three others joined in. But the skipper said:

"Shouts aren't loud enough – nowhere near.
There isn't a hope that they'll hear us from here."

Mr Holler looked at his wife and said:

"Should we, dear?"

There lay little Rory, sleeping peacefully.

"We've got no choice. It's worth a try.
When he wakes up, he's sure to cry!" said Mrs Holler.

Mr Holler gave Rory a prod. The baby woke with a start. His eyes and mouth opened together. This time there were no buns or dummies about to be stuffed in.

The first sound was just a growl. The passengers looked around. Then it was a yell. The passengers shouted:

"Louder! Louder! Keep him awake!
Pinch him! Poke him! Give him a shake!"

Then Rory's yell exploded into an unbelievable, ear-splitting scream. The passengers fell silent. More and more the baby bawled. Had the ship in the distance turned? People stopped waving coats and hankies and put their fingers in their ears. Rory's wailing was like a siren. Was the ship coming towards them? Yes! It was! Rory, the smallest passenger aboard, had saved them all!

The ship pulled alongside. The crew hauled them one by one to safety.

"Three cheers for the baby who's saved the day!" the skipper cried.

"All together now – Hip Hip . . ."

But the 'Hooray' was drowned by Rory's horrendous hollering!

"Bless my barnacles!" said the skipper.

"Yes, well done!

That's a mighty fine fog-horn you have in your son!"

A few days later, back on land, a huge hall was packed with people. At the centre of the stage sat Rory, his two teeth stuck into a toffee apple.

"He's never going to keep quiet through this," said Mrs Holler.

"I wish we'd given today a miss!"

"We are here," the mayor said,
"To present this baby,
With a special award for amazing bravery!"
The mayor held up a medal on a coloured ribbon. Mr Holler held up Rory. He remained wonderfully quiet.

Then, just as the medal was being pinned onto his sailor suit, the pin pricked him. Rory dropped the toffee apple. His mouth flew open.

He shouted and screamed, he bawled and bellowed, he wailed and roared and hooted and howled.

"Say thank you, Rory," his father whispered in his ear.

But by the time Rory was quiet, there was no-one to say thank you *to*.

Everyone but the Hollers had left the hall!